AWN

Seababy

A Little Otter Returns Home

Ellen Levine
illustrated by **Jon Van Zyle**

WALKER & COMPANY
New York

The little otter played in the rolling sea.
His mother fed him,
and cleaned him,
and dried him,
and wrapped him in a seaweed blanket to sleep.

One day the waves beat hard.
The wind whipped the shore,
and the storm separated
the baby otter from his mother.

She called to him,
but the waves drove him away.
He washed up on the beach,
and sand scraped his belly.

The little otter cried out,
but his mother couldn't hear him.

He tilted his nose in the air,
searching for her smell.
It was not there.

Suddenly he was lifted off the sand.
He twisted and squirmed in strange arms
that took him to a place of strange smells.

His mouth was opened, his teeth were touched,
and his fur was pinched and poked.

The little otter was hungry.
"*Whee! Whee!*" he squealed.

He remembered his mother feeding him,
and he drank the special milk quickly.
The little otter burped.

He was put in a pool
that was cool and moved
like the sea on a peaceful day.
Rocking gently, he fell asleep.

The next morning,
the pup splashed and splashed.
It was the sea smell he remembered.

He was lifted up, and the little otter quivered.
What was happening?
Someone rubbed him all over
and scratched his cheeks and his belly.
The thick hairs on his small body
stood up and dried.

He remembered his mother
and how she had scratched his cheeks and belly.
The little otter hummed.

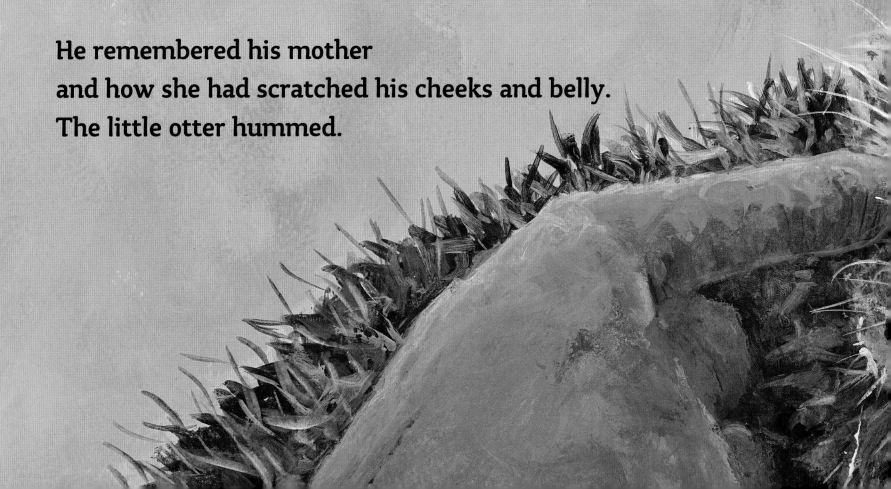

Every day he ate and slept
and played in the water.
Then, one day, he was taken to a bigger pool
where he met his new mom.

She sniffed him.
He sniffed her.
And he was happy.

She dove down for food, and when she came back up, she laid him on her stomach and fed him mussels and clams and crabs.

He learned to dive with her
to the bottom of the pool.
He watched as she reached behind rocks
and pulled out a clam.
Then she reached for another and another.
Together they swam back to the surface.

She put a flat rock on her chest
and broke a clamshell on the rock.
"*Whee! Whee!*" squealed the little otter
as he ate.

Every day they dove together.
Side by side they searched for food.
Side by side they broke the shells.
And side by side they ate.

Sometimes the little otter
looked for food all by himself.
He put a flat rock on his chest all by himself.
He broke open a crab all by himself.
He ate all by himself.

And the little otter hummed.

One day, when he was old enough,
he was ready to leave home.
The little otter was carried to the wide ocean.
He tilted his nose in the air,
and he remembered the smell.

And the little otter hummed.

He rolled over and over and dove down deep.
When he popped up, he saw seagulls flying above.
In the distance, twelve otters floated
on their backs in the seaweed.
They napped and they fluffed their fur.

The little otter swam to them.
He sniffed their backs and they sniffed his.
And he was happy.

That night, surrounded by new friends, he wrapped himself in seaweed and went to sleep.

And so the little otter returned home to the rolling sea.

For Anne —E. L.
For all the adopting mothers, animal and human —J. V. Z.

First published in the United States of America in March 2012
by Walker Publishing Company, Inc., a division of Bloomsbury Publishing, Inc.
www.bloomsburykids.com

For information about permission to reproduce selections from this book, write to
Permissions, Walker BFYR, 175 Fifth Avenue, New York, New York 10010

Library of Congress Cataloging-in-Publication Data
Levine, Ellen.
Seababy / by Ellen Levine ; illustrations by Jon Van Zyle. — 1st U.S. ed.
p.   cm.
Summary: A baby sea otter, separated from his mother by a storm, is rescued by a human who takes him to the
Monterey Bay Aquarium to recover and learn how to take care of himself.
ISBN 978-0-8027-9808-4 (hardcover) • ISBN 978-0-8027-9809-1 (reinforced)
1. Sea otter—Juvenile fiction. [1. Sea otter—Fiction. 2. Otters—Fiction. 3. Animals—Infancy—Fiction. 4. Wildlife
rescue—Fiction. 5. Monterey Bay Aquarium—Fiction. 6. Monterey (Calif.)—Fiction.] I. Van Zyle, Jon, ill. II. Title.
PZ10.3.L556Se 2012   [E]—dc22   2010051082

Art created with acrylic on 300-pound watercolor paper
Typeset in Tyke
Book design by Nicole Gastonguay

Printed in China by C&C Offset Printing Co., Ltd., Shenzhen, Guangdong
(hardcover) 10 9 8 7 6 5 4 3 2 1
(reinforced) 10 9 8 7 6 5 4 3 2 1

All papers used by Bloomsbury Publishing, Inc., are natural, recyclable products made from wood grown in well-
managed forests. The manufacturing processes conform to the environmental regulations of the country of origin.

Acknowledgments

Many thanks to Julie Hymer, who was part of the
early success of the rescue program; and to Karen
Jeffries, the Monterey Bay Aquarium's public relations
manager, for her interest and support. Her help was
invaluable. And to writing buddies Sandra Jordan and
Phyllis Root.

Note to the Reader

The Monterey Bay Aquarium in California has a special program to rescue stranded sea otters. When the staff first began the program, everyone knew they shouldn't handle the wild animals too much because then they couldn't go back to their group in nature. And so the otters were treated by doctors and generally cared for without much touching.

But something wasn't working. When the young otters were released back into the ocean, they didn't know how to find food for themselves in the sea world. They died or were rescued again, to be kept in the aquarium or sent to a zoo.

In nature, otter pups and their moms are very close. The mother teaches the pup everything. And so aquarium workers became "otter moms" to teach the pups what they needed to survive. But even though the staff never talked to the pups, the little ones became too close to humans, and when back in the wild, they tried to connect with surfers and divers.

Today the aquarium staff matches up an orphaned pup with a real otter surrogate mom, who teaches the pup all it needs to know. And like Seababy, the pups are able to go back to their wild ocean world to eat, sleep, play, and roll with the waves.

You can read more about the Monterey Bay Aquarium's Sea Otter Research and Conservation program at:
http://www.montereybayaquarium.org/cr/sorac.aspx

Further Reading and Surfing

BOOKS:

León, Vicki. *A Raft of Sea Otters*. Montrose, CA: London Town Press, 2005.

Smith, Roland. *Sea Otter Rescue*. New York: Puffin, 1999.

Waxman, Laura Hamilton. *Let's Look at Sea Otters*. Minneapolis, MN: Lerner, 2010.

WEBSITES:

Monterey Bay Aquarium has many amazing resources online for you to visit. To reach their general website, which is a gateway to exploring many marine animals and their habitats, visit: http://www.montereybayaquarium.org/

To have the experience of a virtual visit, go to the aquarium's webcam page and pick the animal you want to watch live (including the sea otters): http://www.montereybayaquarium.org/efc/cam_menu.asp

To learn more about the aquarium's sea otter exhibits and resources, visit: http://www.montereybayaquarium.org/efc/otter.aspx

For activities and games about sea otters, visit: http://www.montereybayaquarium.org/lc/teachers_place/activity_otters_busy.asp

To learn more about sea otters in the wild, visit:

http://www.defenders.org/programs_and_policy/wildlife_conservation/imperiled_species/sea_otter/index.php

http://www.marinemammalcenter.org/education/marine-mammal-information/sea-otter.html

http://animals.nationalgeographic.com/animals/mammals/sea-otter.html

To my father

Groundwood Books / House of Anansi Press
110 Spadina Avenue, Suite 801, Toronto, Ontario M5V 2K4
or c/o Publishers Group West
1700 Fourth Street, Berkeley, CA 94710

We acknowledge for their financial support of our publishing program the
Government of Canada through the Canada Book Fund (CBF).

Library and Archives Canada Cataloguing in Publication
Tessler, Tamar, author, illustrator
Abukacha's shoes / written and illustrated by Tamar Tessler.
Issued in print and electronic formats.
ISBN 978-1-55498-458-9 (bound). — ISBN 978-1-55498-459-6 (pdf)
I. Title.
PZ7.T35895Ab 2015   j823'.92   C2014-905800-4
C2014-905801-2

The illustrations are collages, using mixed media.
Design by Michael Solomon
Printed and bound in Malaysia

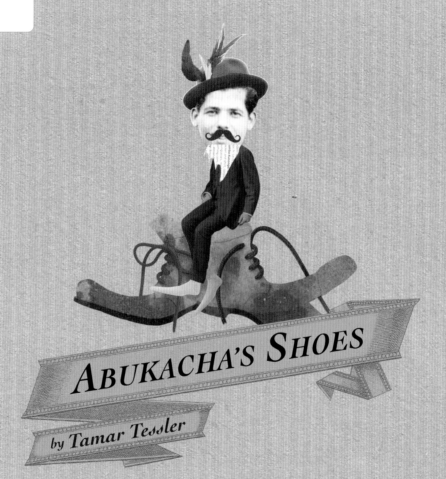

ABUKACHA'S SHOES

by Tamar Tessler

GROUNDWOOD BOOKS
HOUSE OF ANANSI PRESS
TORONTO   BERKELEY

My aunt tells this story about Abukacha and his shoes.

In a little house with a red tile roof, perched on a green hill, in a village far, far away, there lived a man named Abukacha with his wife, Louisa, their son, Schmil, and their old dog, Marco.

Everybody knew Abukacha because he had the biggest shoes in the whole wide world.

Abukacha had bought them long ago. With those shoes, he had worked in the fields, gone fishing, traveled around the world ... and the shoes had become worn out, quite tattered and filthy dirty.

One day Abukacha took a look at his toes poking out of the holes in his shoes, and he realized that the time had come to buy a new pair.

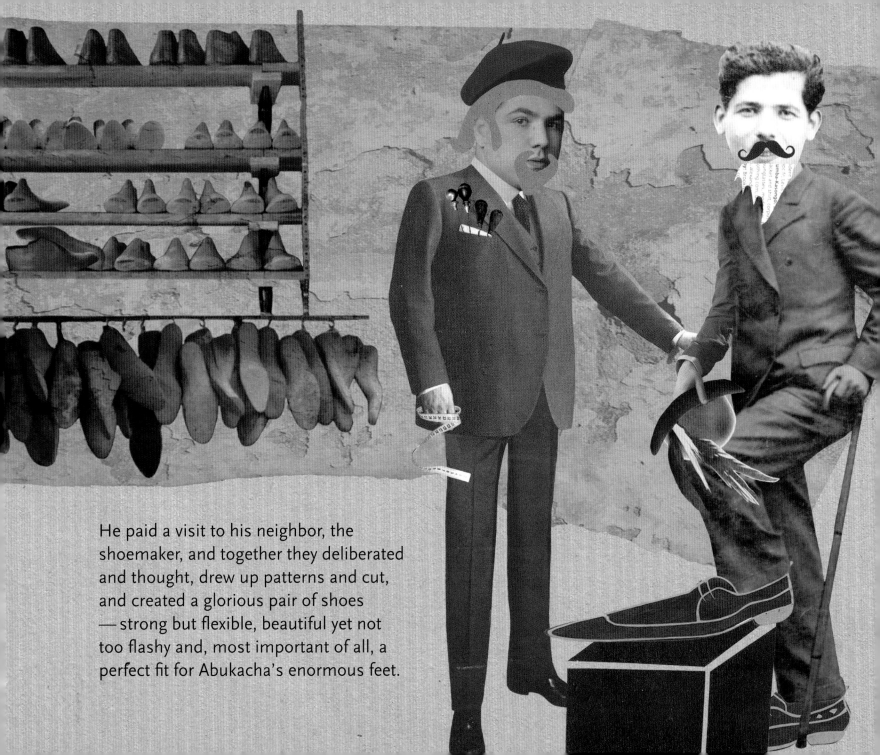

He paid a visit to his neighbor, the shoemaker, and together they deliberated and thought, drew up patterns and cut, and created a glorious pair of shoes —strong but flexible, beautiful yet not too flashy and, most important of all, a perfect fit for Abukacha's enormous feet.

Delighted, Abukacha went home and tossed his old shoes in the garbage can. And as he stretched on the sofa next to Louisa, the two of them gazed happily at the new shoes on Abukacha's feet.

That night, when the garbage truck arrived, the garbage man noticed an enormous pair of shoes bursting out of the can.

"Those must be Abukacha's shoes!" he said. "There's nobody in the world with feet as big as his."

He was sure there had been a mistake.

When Abukacha woke up the next morning, he found, to his great surprise, the old pair of shoes on his doorstep.

"Maybe my shoes were too big to fit in the garbage truck," Abukacha said to himself.

That very afternoon, he loaded his old shoes onto his bicycle and, with his son, Schmil, rode to the seashore. There Abukacha tied the shoes to a big rock and tossed them into the sea.

Then he sat next to his son on a large boulder, and as the sun was setting he said his last goodbyes to the sinking shoes.

Several days later, on a bright spring morning, a fisherman thought he had caught a huge fish on his rod. But much to his disappointment, when he reeled in the line he saw two gigantic shoes hanging off the hook.

"Those must be Abukacha's shoes!" he exclaimed. "There's nobody in the world with feet as big as his."

And so it happened, later that day, Abukacha saw a green truck with his old shoes heading for his house.

"Somebody dumped your shoes into the sea!"
the fisherman said, placing them on the ground.

Abukacha and Louisa gazed in confusion at the
wet shoes.

"There has got to be a way to get rid of these old
shoes," said Abukacha crossly.

Fastening his shoes to the roof rack of his car, Abukacha traveled for a week with his old dog, Marco, until they reached a far-off, secluded village whose name he didn't know. And at the edge of that village, he found a deep well and threw the old shoes down into its depths. When Abukacha heard the dull thud of the shoes hitting the water, he returned to his car and went back home with a huge sense of relief.

As fate would have it, on that very same day, into that very same well, fell a doll that belonged to a little girl — the daughter of the village mayor.

The townspeople gathered around the well as they dropped a long, thick rope down its side. And just when it seemed that the iron hook had snagged the doll's dress, and the rescuers slowly, slowly pulled up the rope, everyone was disappointed to see the gigantic shoes dangling at its end.

"Those must be Abukacha's shoes!" someone shouted. "There's nobody in the world with feet as big as his."

Days later, Louisa and Abukacha gazed in disbelief when a farmer arrived with the pair of old shoes.

"There has got to be a way to get rid of these shoes!" muttered Abukacha.

There was a long silence, and then Louisa suggested a solution. From the damp attic, they pulled out the hot-air balloon they had received for their wedding and took it out to the backyard. They tied the tattered old shoes to the wicker basket, lit the burner and released the balloon high into the air.

When morning dawned, Abukacha woke up with an odd feeling. Upon opening his front door, he found nothing but a rolled-up newspaper on his doorstep. He sat outside, leafed through the newspaper and threw an occasional glance towards the path leading to his house.

Nobody came. No car passed along the dirt road.

Abukacha looked down at his new, clean shoes, and something gnawed at his heart. He jumped into a dirty puddle in the garden, ran across the muddy field and walked back and forth over the sharp cobblestones — but his shoes remained nice and new, shiny and intact.

Tired and wistful, he lay among the flowers to take a nap.

My aunt can't explain how it happened, but when Abukacha woke up, just before the sun began to set, he noticed a colorful spot in the sky slowly heading towards him. And as Abukacha watched the hot-air balloon and his old shoes float to a landing near the daffodils in his garden, he understood that this was where his shoes belonged and this was where they would stay.

AUTHOR'S NOTE

When I was a little girl, my aunt Haya would tell me the story of Abukacha and his shoes — a folktale she herself heard as a child from her aunt Fella. The plot was always different, but the problem remained the same — Abukacha had the biggest shoes in the world, and he couldn't get rid of them no matter what he did.

In a world that exists beyond time and space, I tried to explore my childhood memories and my family's history — mixing the old with the new and fiction with documentary.

Containing photos of my grandmother's Polish family, this book commemorates her mother, father, brothers and sisters who perished in the Holocaust.

The Jewish-Ukrainian poet Zelda wrote, "Each person has a name." My hope is that this book will bring these people back to life, if only for a second, and remind us all that every name has a face and a life of its own.

This book is also dedicated to my mother, Rina, my aunt Haya and my uncle Gideon — the Neubergs.

And to my loved ones Teo and Haim.

I wish to thank the wonderful people of House of Anansi and Groundwood Books — Sarah MacLachlan, Sheila Barry, Michael Solomon and Nan Froman — for making this project come to life.

Special thanks to Haya Harareet Clayton, Haim Tabakman, Maya Arad, Aliza Raz Melzer, Emi Sfard, Ady Levy and Naomi Amit.